EliBC

BLACKBERRY FARM

A BUNNY IN TROUBLE

Jane Pilgrim

This edition first published in the United Kingdom in 2000 by
Brockhampton Press
20 Bloomsbury Street
London WC1B 3QA
a member of the Caxton Publishing Group

Designed and Produced for Brockhampton Press by
Open Door Limited
80 High Street, Colsterworth, Lincolnshire, NG33 5JA

Illustrator: F. Stocks May
Colour separation: GA Graphics Stamford

Title: BLACKBERRY FARM, A Bunny in Trouble
ISBN: 1-84186-038-7

Printed in Singapore by Star Standard Industries Pte. Ltd.

A BUNNY IN TROUBLE

Jane Pilgrim

Illustrated by F. Stocks May

BROCKHAMPTON PRESS

It was a lovely sunny morning at Blackberry Farm, and Mr Nibble counted the lettuces in his garden. "One, two, three, four, five–" and all ready to eat. One for himself, one for Mrs Nibble, and one for each of his children, Rosy, Posy and Christopher.

In the kitchen, Mrs Nibble gave
the little bunnies their breakfast.
"After school," she said, "we will
go for a picnic. So hurry home as
fast as you can."

Rosy, Posy and Christopher went to the school kept by Ernest Owl. They were good little bunnies, and did their lessons very well. But that morning Posy could not get her sum right, and Ernest Owl was very cross. "You must stay in and do it again," he said, and sent all the others home.

Poor Posy was very sad. She would miss the picnic. She sat on her little stool and dripped large tears on to her little paws. Ernest Owl went outside to light his pipe, and she was left alone.

Rosy and Christopher told Mr
and Mrs Nibble what had
happened. But the picnic was
packed and they decided to go.
Lucy Mouse, who had come to
help Mrs Nibble that morning,
said she would wait for Posy and
look after her.

So off the party went, and
Mr Nibble carried the lettuces in a
big bag on his shoulder.

They all came home at tea-time. There sat Lucy Mouse all alone. "Where is little Posy?" Mrs Nibble cried. Lucy Mouse heaved a big sigh and said, "I do not know. I have waited here all the time and she has not come home."

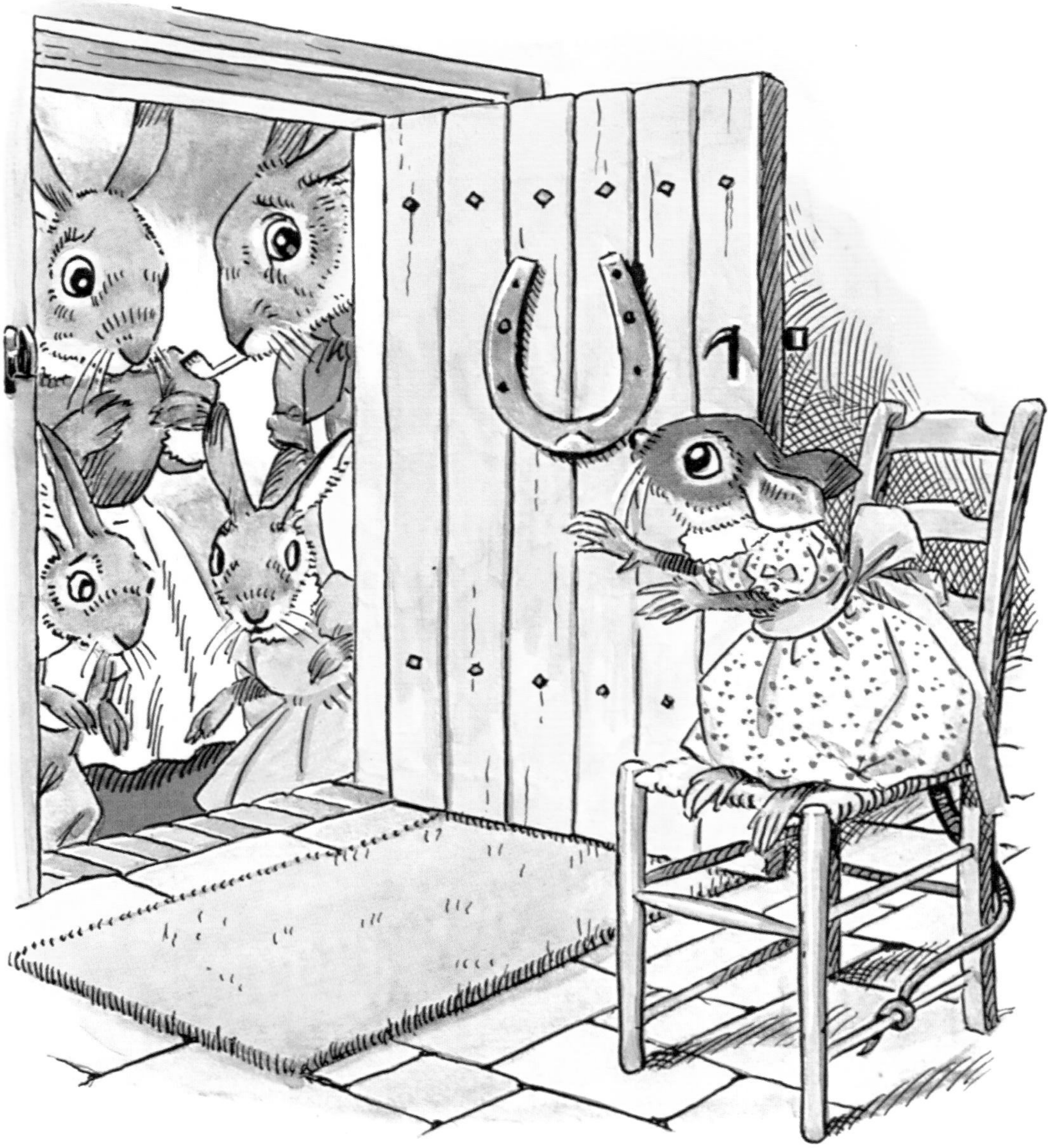

Mr Nibble set off at once for the school. But there was no one there. The door was shut, and Ernest Owl had gone home. Mr Nibble was very worried. He was afraid that Posy must be lost.

But Posy was not lost. Kind Joe
Robin had come to help her with
her sum. "Thank you, Joe," Posy
had said, "It is very kind of you.
But I have missed my picnic party
and there will be no one at home
for me to play with." And a large
tear rolled down her nose on to
her dress.

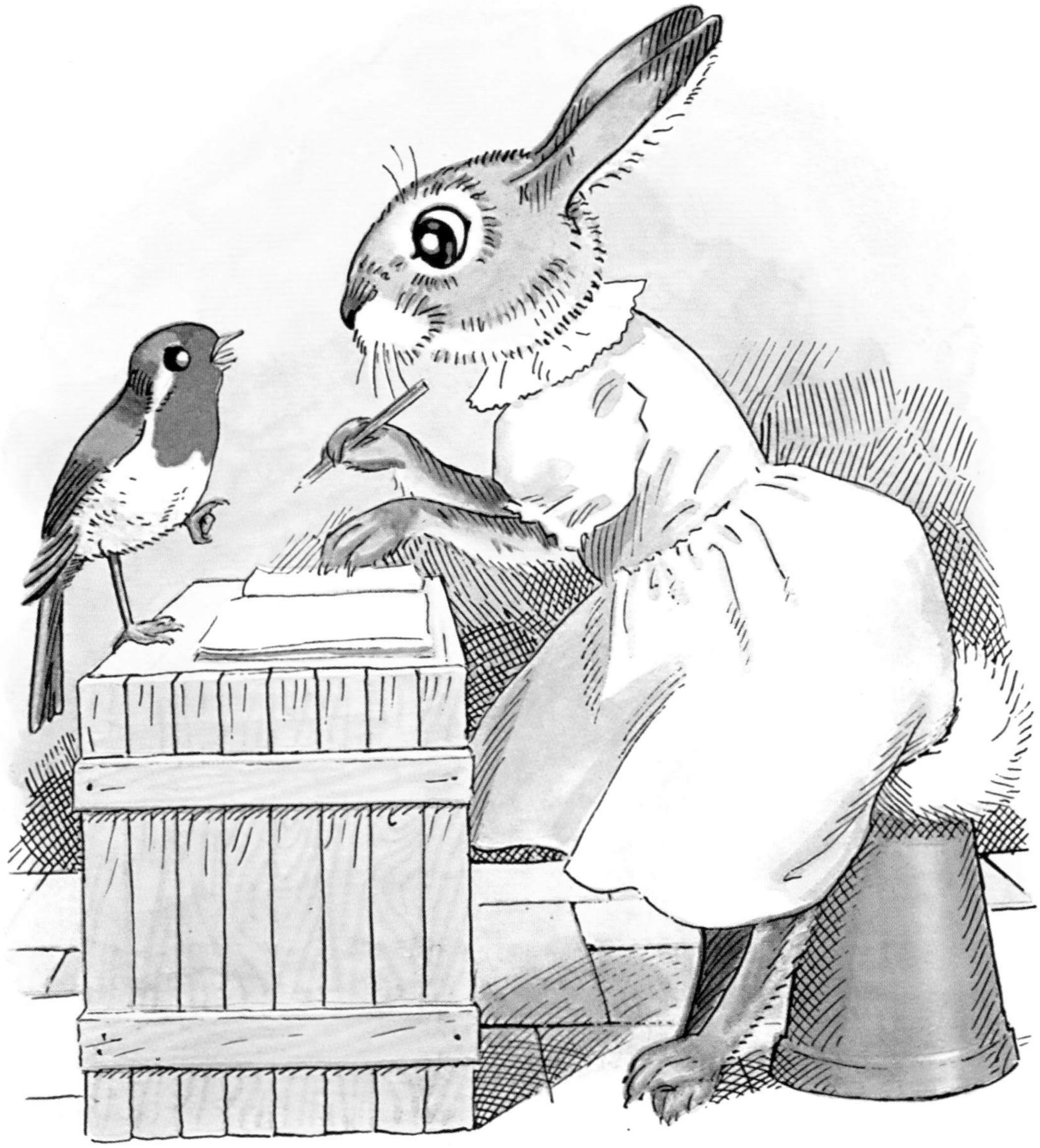

Joe Robin said, "never mind, Posy. I am going to see Mrs Squirrel and Hazel. You shall come too. Show your sum to Ernest Owl, and we will go."

So Posy showed her sum to Ernest Owl, and he said, "You are a good girl. Now you can go home."

"I am going out with Joe Robin," she said. "If you see my mummy, will you tell her?" and she hopped off happily with her friend.

Mrs Squirrel and Hazel were
very pleased to see them and gave
them a lovely lunch sitting under
a big oak tree.

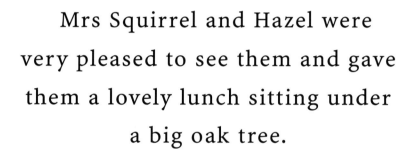

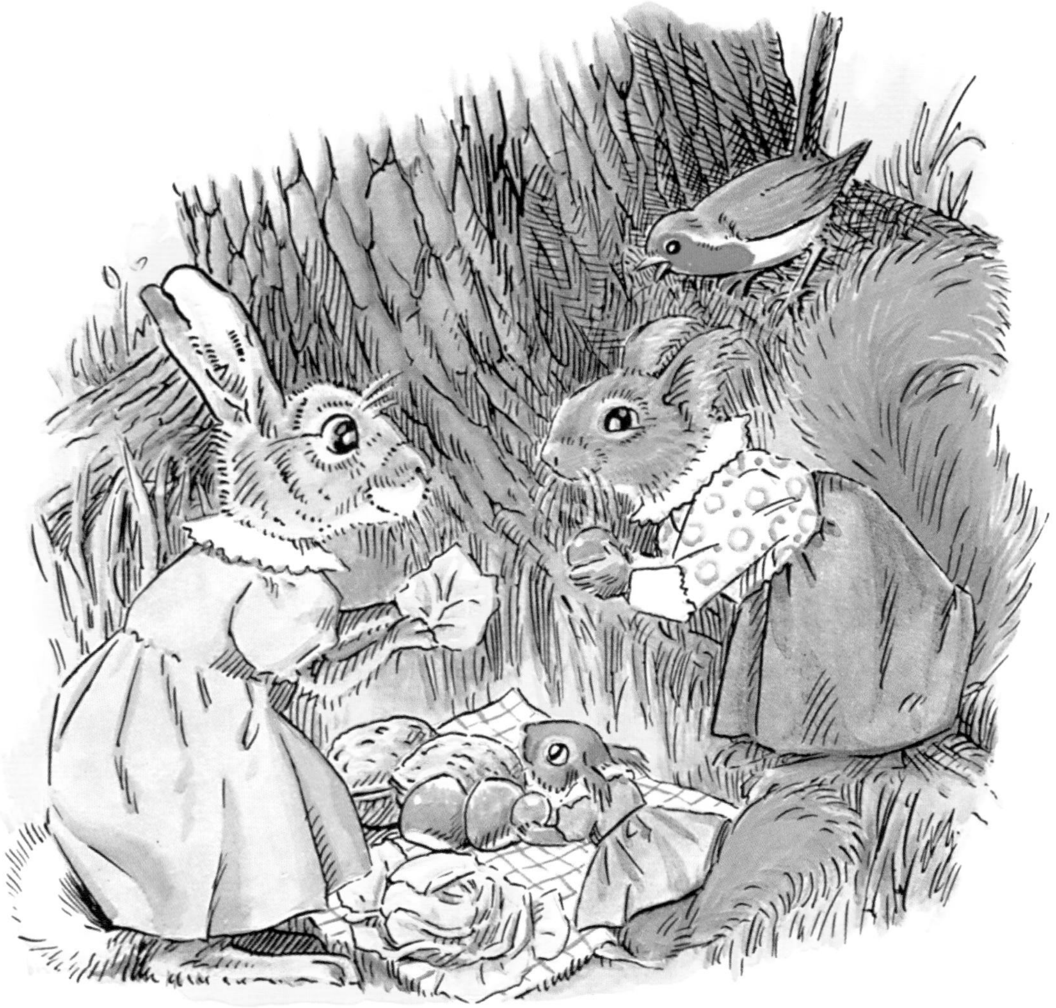

Ernest Owl left a note outside
the school,

"Dear Mrs Nibble,
Posy has gone with Joe Robin
Love from
Ernest Owl."

But Mr Nibble did not see it,
because Ernest Owl put it too high
up. So he went sadly home thinking
that his little Posy was lost.

But when he got home he found Posy and Joe Robin waiting for him on the doorstep, and Mrs Nibble making another pot of tea. Posy told him about the very difficult sum and how Joe Robin had helped her and looked after her. "Thank you, Joe Robin, very much," said Mr Nibble. "I don't know how we should all manage without you at Blackberry Farm."

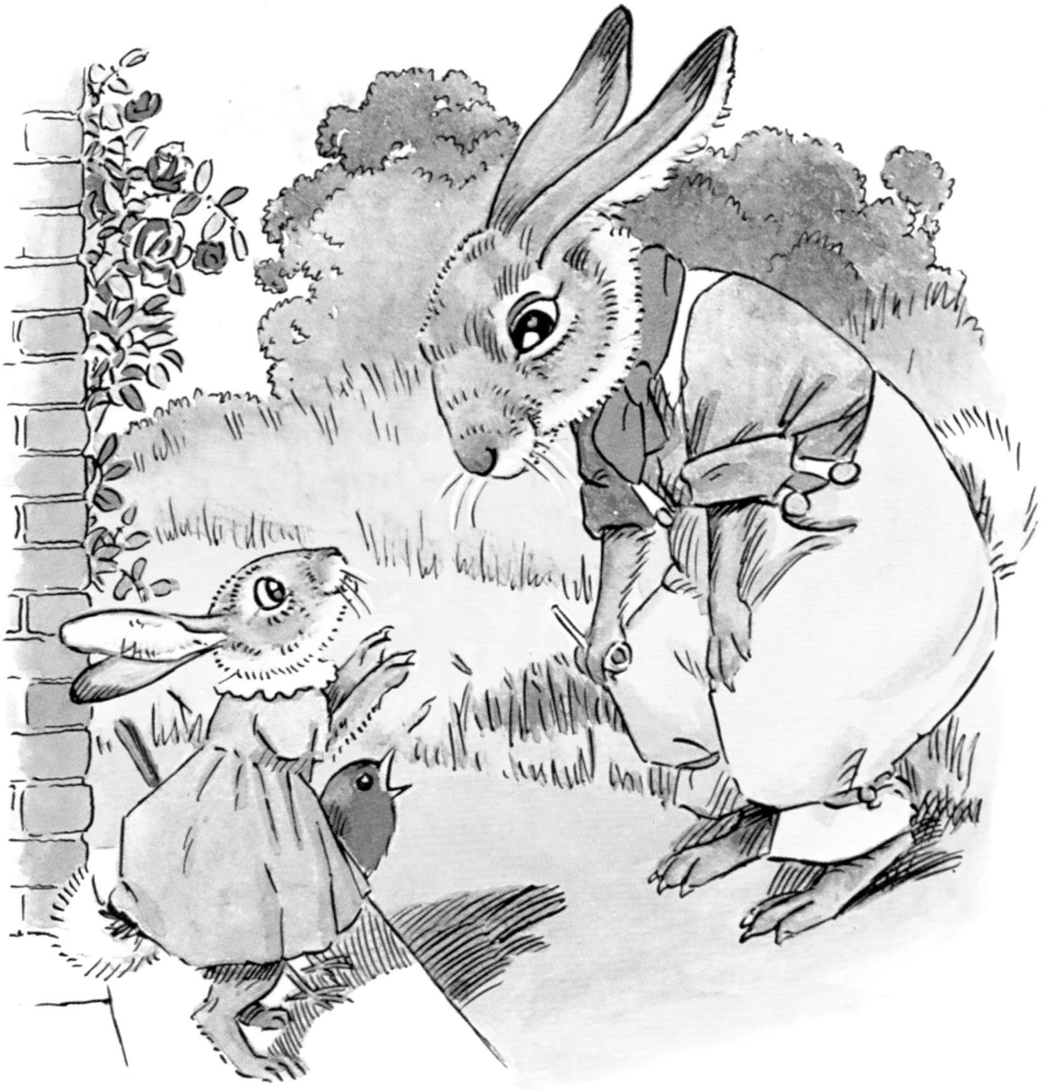

Then he hugged Posy very tight, and Mrs Nibble fetched the very special lettuce they had saved for her, and everyone was happy. "We shall have another picnic another day," said Mr Nibble, "and Joe Robin must come as well." And they all thought that was a splendid idea.

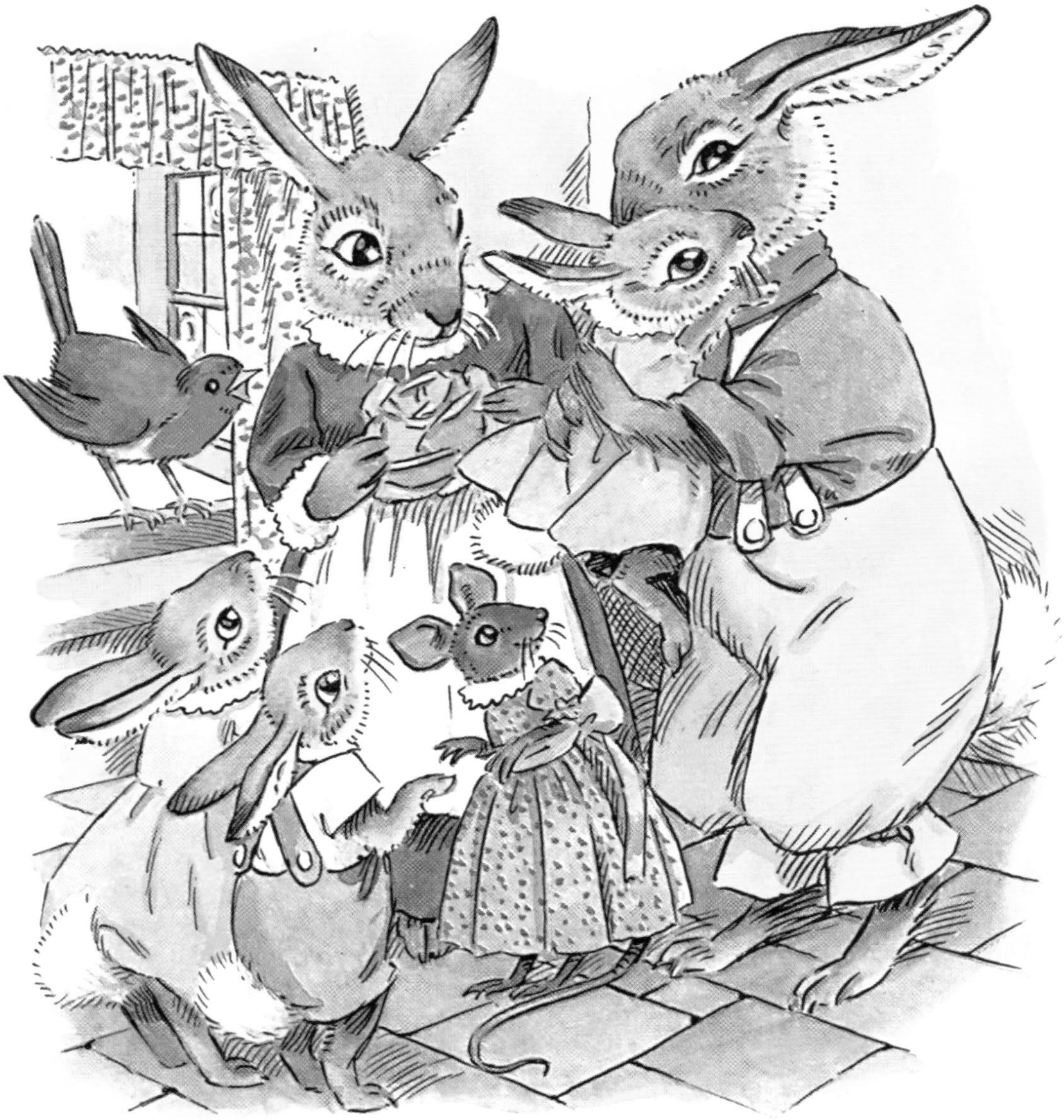

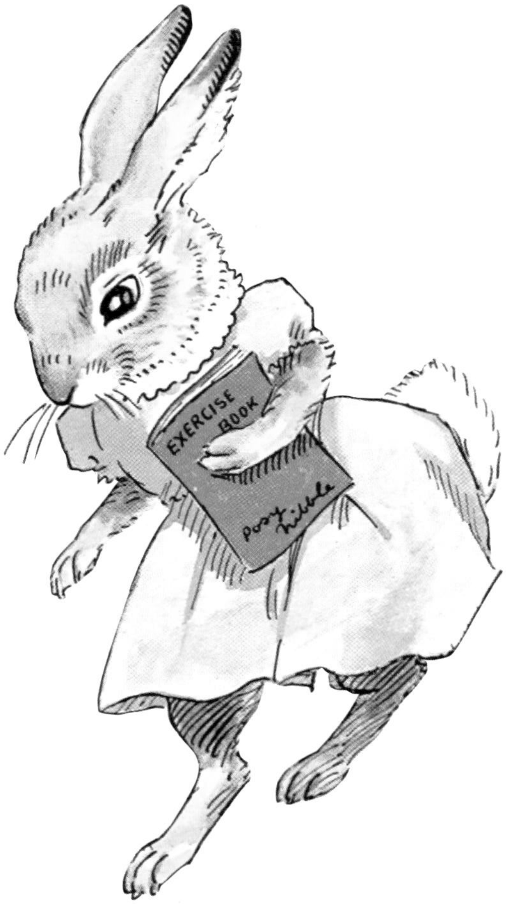
EXERCISE BOOK